Vengeance

Ryan Mundy

Cover Design: izabeladesigns

Editing: Susan Keillor

Proofreading: Susan Keillor

Paperback ISBN: 979-8-9877506-5-0

Music

Soulmate – Chanin
Paint The Town Red – Dojo Cat
High – Caitlyn Smith
Chemtrails Over the Country Club – Lana Del Ray
Breathe Me – Sia

To those that said I wouldn't become something.
Fuck you.

BLURB

Salem

I was supposed to be okay.

He was the end of my past, he was a means to an end. But when I finally end his life, I'm lost.

I don't know who I am. I'm no longer a person. I'm no longer living. I'm nothing but a void now.

Zane

She's lost. Her mind is gone, leaving behind a fragile girl who doesn't know who she is.

And I have no idea how to help her.

Content Warning

Graphic Sexual Scene

Torture

Murder

Physical Assault

Depression and suicidal thoughts

Past trauma

Note from author

Vengeance is a continuance of Psychological War. Though the book ended with a HEA, this short story closes it officially.

While Love and War, along with Red Obsession is not following the same love interest, it's still recommend to reads those first.

Order -

Psychological War

Love and War

Red Obsession

Vengeance

If you do not wish to read Love and War, Red Obsession, you might be a little confused on how they found Luca. It can be found in the end of Red Obsession. Go read and find out.

1

Salem

"Spit on my cock, Kitten," Zane orders me. Smirking up at him between his legs, I try my best to create more saliva before spitting on him like he orders. "Good girl," he smirks. I give him no warning, taking him back into my mouth. My throat swallows around his head causing him to thrust his hips, groaning and losing his control.

God, I would never get over this man. Everything about him lights my body on fire. Snapping my eyes up, Zane is already staring down at me, his hands fisted in the sheets. I smile the best I can with my mouth being full.

Suddenly he grabs a fistful of my hair, yanking me off him. "Come up here, Kitten."

My body can't move fast enough. I'm climbing him faster than I've ever moved in my life. Placing my hands on the headboard, I hover over his face, watching as he raises his pierced eyebrow at me. I smile back as I place myself directly over his waiting mouth.

Zane loves being smothered by me. If I wasn't sitting directly on his face, putting all my weight down, he would growl and force me. Not that I don't love it.

I do.

I love everything with him.

His tongue latches onto my clit, causing me to make inhumane moans. I'm losing my mind with the way he's moving his tongue against me. My eyes begin to close as I'm chasing my orgasm. It's so close. It's right th–

Then I'm lifted up and thrown down onto my back. But I don't have a chance to protest before Zane is lining himself up at my entrance. His arms are on either side of my head, caging me in. Pressing forward, our gazes lock as he enters me.

"Fuck," he growls. I can't stop myself from grabbing his face, pressing my lips against his. I thrust my tongue into his mouth, tasting myself. Zane growls, his groin flushing with mine, our tongues fighting for dominance.

I gasp as he pulls himself out slowly, before thrusting in again.

"You're so fucking perfect." he groans against my mouth. I get no warning as he picks up speed, placing his head against my neck. I hold on for dear life, as he pounds into me. I'm sure to have bruises.

"Fuck, fuck, fuck," I chant, my clit becoming oversensitive from the drag of his pubic bone against it. My orgasm comes out of nowhere, my nails digging into his back, dragging down. I'm sure I'm drawing blood.

I whimper into his mouth, our foreheads smashed together as he moves inside me. Picking up his pace, my pelvis meeting his thrust, I try to circle my hips. Needing to get him closer, deeper.

"Shit," Zane moans, circling his arms around my head, holding on for dear life.

"Fuck my ass," I groan into his ear. Zane and I have done anal a few times, and usually he's the one initiating it. But right now, I want him to. Oh, God, do I want him to so much.

"You're serious?" His movements slow, his eyes searching mine. I try moving my hips again, not wanting him to stop. "Salem," he growls.

"Yes, yes, I'm serious, Zane. Own my ass," I smirk. Knowing if I tell him to own this, he'll gladly do it.

"Hands and knees." He pulls out. Barely giving me time to do as he says, his hands are grabbing my ass, pulling my cheeks apart. It's dirty and wrong, but fuck, do I love it.

"Fuck," he grunts. Peering at him over my shoulder, our eyes connect as he spits on my asshole. His thumb rubs circles around my clit, turning me into a moaning mess. Fuck, this man and his hands. Dragging my pussy juice up to my ass, he rubs, smearing his saliva and my juices together. Bending down he keeps eye contact as he licks a slow trail pussy to asshole.

"Fu-fuck." I nearly drop my body onto the mattress. Placing a finger against me, he suddenly pushes, and my muscles finally give way. "Oh, *God.*"

"There's no God here, only a monster, ready to defile his pretty whore." Zane's voice is rough, his tongue prodding me over and over again. Pressing against the middle of my back, my chest hits the mattress, my ass in the air. "Such a pretty little hole."

God this man and his mouth.

Two fingers and I'm a moaning mess.

Three fingers and I can barely control my breathing.

Four fingers and I'm so full.

I swear I can't handle much more, and it's not until he removes his hands that they're quickly replaced by his cock. Pushing forward, he's met with resistance.

"Relax, Kitten." Zane coos, reaching around he pinches my clit. I nearly buckle when he plunges two fingers into my pussy. Easing his cock into my ass, I relax as much as I can with his two fingers scissoring my pussy and his slow thrust in my ass. "Move your ass back," he demands.

I shake my head into the mattress, sweat slipping down my back. I hiss as he smacks my ass, adding another finger to my pussy. "I *said* push back," Zane grunts.

Taking a deep breath, I push back, shoving the rest of his cock deep into me.

"Holy fuck." He squeezes my ass cheeks, spreading them wide as he slips his cock out until the tip nearly slips and then thrusts back in. "That's my girl, taking my fat cock like a good girl."

Three fingers push into my cunt. I'm moaning so loud it's inhuman. Tears stream down my face when I'm suddenly being lifted up, and my back slams against his chest. Bowing my back, he continues thrusting into me like a man on death row.

"You're squeezing me, you like me *owning* this ass, don't you?" I try to nod, only I can't move or answer, especially when that hand that was deep in my cunt is now prying my mouth open and shoved into my mouth. Drool spills down my chin. "I asked you a question, Kitten, answer me!"

"YES!" I scream around his fingers. My orgasm rips me apart. I see stars, and my body shakes. My hands grip his arm, the only thing holding me up. Liquid pours from my cunt, Zane's hand rubbing faster and faster as my soul wrecks my body and leaves.

Death by squirt.

"Shhhh," Zane's voice barely reaches my ears. "You're wonderful," he murmurs into my ear. I'm vaguely aware of him helping me lay on my side and pulling the covers over us. He slowly slips from me, causing me to wince slightly.

His body presses against me as he eases my legs apart. There's no way I can handle any more, I barely have any energy left. Just as I open my mouth to tell him to fuck off before I remove his balls, he places a warm damp cloth against me, cleaning between my legs.

"*Oh.*" I sigh in relief. That feels so nice.

"You did so well," he praises. I vaguely hear the cloth being tossed across the room before he eases his way in behind me. Rubbing my thigh, I drift off to sleep.

I jolt awake, heart pounding against my chest as my body jerks itself up. My hands clutch the covers against my chest, and my body breaks out in sweat, my eyes slamming shut.

"Sa–" My fist shoots out connecting with whatever poor bastard decided to lie next to me. "Salem!" *Zane.* Double shit.

My eyes adapt to the dim lighting in our room, when I finally see Zane covering his face with his hands.

"Fuck," I mumble, crawling to him. Removing his hands from his face, I move into his lap and cup his cheek. Thankfully, he's not bleeding, but I know my punches hurt. "I'm so–"

"I'm okay," he whispers, kissing my nose.

Smiling at him, I nod my head, not bothering with trying to argue with him. We used to argue for hours until finally we both realized most of the time it was a waste of time. We are both stubborn assholes.

"Nightmare." It wasn't a question, he knew. Though they are farther and farther apart. I still have them, and sometimes they woke me up, which causes me to throw punches and ask questions later.

I tried telling him to sleep in a different bed. But he refuses, and that was one of our first arguments. Went on for days it seemed, until finally he made me realize even if we weren't legally married, I was his, and that includes my past. And the part where I might break a nose every now and then. Thankfully, it's been a few months since I've broken his nose last.

"Do you ever think of them?" I whisper, unable to look at him directly. We never talk much about his parents. To think about it, we've only talked about them twice. Zane usually steers the conversation elsewhere.

"Was it about them?" he asks back. Clearly not wanting to talk about his own parents. I roll my eyes, trying to wiggle off him. But Zane is not having that. Pressing against my back he throws me back so he's now lying over me. Moving himself between my legs, his arms trap my head. Now I'm forced to look at him directly or close my eyes.

"Sometimes I feel like they would be disappointed in me. More my father than Mom, but then I remember that even though they barely raised me because they were so focused on their own career, they wanted me to be selfless, to help others."

"You are very selfless," I mumble. I know I sound sarcastic, but I'm not trying to be. Zane is probably one of the least selfish people I know. Sure, he's an asshole. But he's always helping others, in a weird killer way.

"Mom wanted me to marry someone I loved. She didn't care who she was, only that I loved her and treated her well. Dad tried setting me up a few times with some girls from the country club."

I couldn't stop the eyeroll. From the sound of what his father wanted, I definitely do not fit what he wanted for his son.

"Sure, I think of them, but our relationship was strained in the end. I miss them, but I have to think about the fact we probably wouldn't talk if they were here." Kissing my nose, I close my eyes giving into the smile.

"I don't think your parents would accept me," I mumble.

"Why?"

"Zane, look at me," I huff.

Of course, Zane sits back on his knees, his eyes traveling down my naked form. I used to be insecure about my scars, my body is literally littered with them.

"Zane." I try not to make it sound like I moan his name, but something is obviously wrong with my voice.

Smirking at me, my eyes snap down to his groin, watching as he begins to harden, *again.*

"I am looking at you and I'm a little confused on what you mean by *I don't think your parents would accept me, look at me.*" Mocking me, I fist my hand, punching him in the shoulder.

Zane grunts, rubbing where I punched him. Narrowing his eyes at me, I'm hauled up, his arms wrapping around my back. I can feel his cock pressing against my entrance, and then he's pressing into me.

"You know what I see?"

"Hmmm?" My eyes close as I rock my hips, unable to stop myself.

Resting his hands on my hips, I circle my arms around his neck, crossing my legs behind his back.

"I see a woman who puts everyone's needs before her own. I see a woman who went through trauma and though she could've given up, she didn't and got revenge for her family. I see someone who is strong physically and mentally. Someone who is beautiful and wonderful, and so fucking hot." Pushing my hips back and then bringing me forward I whimper, needing him. "I see someone who I love, and I would do absolutely anything for."

Leaving me no chance to respond, Zane captures my lips, thrusting his tongue into my mouth. His hands are tightening on my hips, pushing and pulling me faster than I can handle.

It takes no time for both of us to lose ourselves in each other. Losing our minds before we collapse back into bed.

Dumping a cup of stick butter into the mixer, I turn it on as I begin pouring a cup of light brown sugar, and then half a cup of white sugar. Waiting for it to finish mixing, I turn the mixer off before adding one egg at a time and then the vanilla.

"I've gained more weight since I met you than I thought I would," Zane says walking into the kitchen. Glaring up, I ignore his comment as I continue until the butter is smooth before adding the flour mixture.

Ever since I was little, I used to bake with Mama. It had become my coping mechanism. It was something that brought me joy and felt like I was close to her even if I wasn't.

It's not until Zane's arm wraps around my waist that I realize I'm just staring at the mixer, unable to turn it on.

"What's going on inside that pretty head of yours?" he asks.

Shrugging, I ignore the heartache. Turning the mixer on, I reach for the oats before pouring a good amount in.

"Just thinking about them," I mumble. "Sometimes I just wonder what life would be like if they were here."

Spinning me around, Zane shuts the mixer off. Picking me up, he sets me down on the counter, resting his hands on my thighs.

"You don't have to do this," he mumbles, searching my face.

"I do. Nuh, let me explain. I didn't think. When I was going after them, I wanted revenge, so I went for it. I almost gave up the idea of catching Luca. I let myself give up the idea that I was moving on. But now what if I can't go through with it? What if I freak out? What does that say about me?"

"That you're human, Salem."

He just doesn't understand. What if I freeze when I see him? What if I get flashbacks to that night? Sure, I have nightmares about it, but they are fewer and far between. Zane is always there. He never complains when I wake up swinging, when I punch and kick him because I'm trying to get away from those monsters. Instead, he holds me, soothes me. Lets me cry and reminds me that he won't let anyone hurt me.

I believe him. It took me a while to know he wouldn't hurt me, that he isn't going to walk out the door when things get tough. But I believe him.

"I miss them so much." I choke on a sob. I don't mean to cry, to break down, but *fuck*. I miss them so much. "I miss them so much it hurts, Zane."

"I know, I know."

Dropping my head onto his chest, I let myself feel and I cry. I cry so hard, my body shakes. But Zane just holds me against his chest, his hand rubbing circles into my back. Comforting me.

"They'd be proud of you," he says, kissing the top of my head.

"I'm a killer, how could they be proud of that?"

"You protect those who need it. You care deeply, and Salem," he says, cupping my cheeks. "Look at me, I'm going to be right there with you. I'm not going anywhere."

Nodding my head slightly, I wait.

"Remember you had the same feeling when you met Emilia for the first time? You thought you were going to freak out because of Toby, and you didn't. You did so fucking well." Pressing his lips against mine, I let out a sigh of relief.

"I love you."

"I love you," he mumbles against my mouth. Stepping back, he claps his hands together. "Alright, let's bake some cookies!"

Laughing, I jump down from the counter, and we do exactly that.

2

Zane

I could cum just looking at Salem. Literally.

The way her outfit hugs her glorious ass, the way I can see her nipples through her thin leather catsuit. She's a wet fucking dream and *fuck.* The way she bends over, *her pussy is wide open, and I could fit my thick cock into her tight fucking puss–*

"Zane," Salem snaps. I shake my head, clearing my thoughts of wanting to fuck Salem right here on the stairs. "I swear if you don't stop staring at my ass, I'm going to tie you to the fucking chair and torture you instead."

"Don't threaten me with a good time, Kitten." Dragging my hand over my stubbled chin, Salem rolls her eyes at me, sharpening her knife.

And fuck, she looks hot. She could literally stab me, and I'd probably beg her to do it again.

"You think I'm joking. I'll tie you to the chair, Zane."

"And you think I won't like it," I mutter, grabbing her hips, bending down to kiss her neck. Suddenly Salem is swinging around, knocking my feet from under me. Landing on my back, she places her bare foot against my throat. Groaning, I grip her ankle, dragging it up until I kiss the arch of her foot.

"Zane," Salem growls.

"Kitten." Meeting her eyes, Salem tries her hardest to be upset with me, but we both know she's loving this.

"You're not supposed to be distracting me. I have a job *to do*," she moans as my hand massages into her heel. "Stop, you can play with my feet later. I might even let you suck my toes, you weirdo."

Laughing she moves her foot off me, backing up. Getting to my feet, I grip her hips once more, peering around her shoulders.

"You're still nervous," I state. After Salem woke up from her nightmare, I tried distracting her by making cookies. Her favorite pastime besides taking her horse Pumpkin out. It worked for a little before she was rambling on about not being able to go through with ending his life. I don't know why she feels like she can't. She's killed countless men, and she never thought about it. And I didn't understand why all of a sudden, she is.

But Salem overthinks.

A lot.

When we first met, I would never have guessed she would. But Salem gets overwhelmed by nearly everything in life. She has more issues than she ever lets on, that I'm sure Aziza, her best friend, doesn't even know about.

She feels like everyone is going to abandon her.

Though it wasn't her family's choice, they were taken from her. Killed and raped in front of her, while she was stabbed, throat slit, and left for dead. My girl is strong, and she survived.

Then trained for nine years and took those lives that took her family from her.

All but one.

"Is it bad that I just want to get it over with?" she asks, dropping the knife before picking up another one.

"No, it's not bad. He took them from you, and while you want him to feel the same pain you did, he's not going to. He never will. You can torture him, but he knows eventually you're going to kill him. He knows he won't be getting out of here alive. But that doesn't mean you can't play with him." I shrug. Another thing I've gotten good at while living here besides taking care of the farm, is Salem always needs pep talks. Which is odd. I thought I knew who she was back then. That was all a lie. Salem is a quiet nerd, who likes baking and watching Disney movies.

Over and over again.

"One day. I'll take it out of him for one day. Then I'll be done." She nods her head, agreeing to whatever else is inside her head.

"That's all you need, Kitten." Kissing the side of her head, Salem leans into me.

"Alright, play time." Salem smiles, reaching for her boots. She slips them on and takes off towards the side door in the basement.

My crazy fucking girl.

Strolling over, I step inside, closing the door behind me. Even though she doesn't have any neighbors, sometimes Miss Elena comes over to drop off fresh eggs or baked bread. I think she knows what Salem does, but I've never gotten the nerve to ask.

A muffled scream brings my attention back. Arms tied to the arm rest, legs tied to the legs, spread wide. He sits there in nothing, naked as the day he was born. Beside the little fabric tied around his mouth holding his boxers in his mouth.

Luca fucking Russo.

"My name," Salem's voice goes emotionless. The way she always does when she goes after those men. She doesn't believe she can numb her feelings, but always does.

Luca shakes his head, refusing to say anything. Not that he can say much with his boxers shoved down his throat. Salem moves around the room, pulling a cart over.

I can't see what she's grabbing, but Luca begins shaking his head. Eyes wide, trying his best to move back in the chair. Unluckily for him, I've screwed that chair in enough that even I couldn't move from it. And I'm twice the size of him.

"I'll ask once more, my name." Salem stands in front of Luca, waiting.

He mumbles something that I'm doubting was her name. Salem must have thought the same because she plunges whatever is in her hand into his thigh.

"I didn't quite hear you there, what's my name!" Ripping the rope and boxers from his mouth, he screams at the top of his lungs.

"S–stop," he begs.

"That's not what I fucking asked!" Dragging the weapon across, blood squirting from his legs, she says, "here's an easier one, what's my mother's name?"

"Em–Emily."

"Very good, very good." Placing the weapon back onto the cart, I finally see it was a screwdriver. "I want to know why. See since I was little, I've had this question wrapped around my brain. I try to understand, can you believe it?" Salem laughs. "A fucking nine-year-old trying to understand why a group of monster, not men, because men don't rape and murder people for their own fucking pleasure!" she screams.

I don't want to correct her that I murder people for pleasure but decide against it. When she gets like this, there's no telling what she might do. Like stab me in the eye.

"I–I'm sorry," Luca stutters out. It only makes Salem angry, and seconds later she's grabbing what looks like—*fuck is that a fishing hook?* Gripping his hair, she shoves his head back, holding the hook over his eyes.

"Sorry? You're fucking sorry?"

Plunging the hook into his eyes, she literally hooks the fucker's eyeball. I cringe, my left eye twitching as I watch Salem laugh at Luca trying to get her off him.

Tugging the hook back out, she makes sure to twist and rip half his eye out. I'm sure the fucker is going to bleed out.

"Oh, fuck, right, *sorry.*"

The one thing I love about my girl is how petty she can be. Luca screams, his body squirming.

"Oh, shit, I hope he isn't dead yet." She pouts, her lip actually sticking out as she glances at me over her shoulder.

"One day, Kitten," I remind her.

"One day, Cinnamon Roll."

Rolling my eyes at her stupid nickname for me, I pull a chair up crossing my leg over the other and watch as my girl wrecks and tortures Luca. A few times I can't hold my wince, like when she plucks his already half eye and forces him to eat it. Then there was the cheese grater she took to his... dick. It was currently hanging on by a small piece of skin.

I swear my own shriveled up and has yet to drop.

She carves, slices, and burns.

Luca holds on longer than I gave him credit for. But five hours later, Salem drags her favorite knife across his throat. I'm not sure if he's even aware of what's happening. His head hangs back, his throat flayed open.

"I feel better," Salem declares, walking towards me looking very Carrie-like after the bloodbath.

Grabbing her hand, I open the side door and tug her towards the bathroom she has down here. Dropping her hand, I turn the shower on, hot since she loves practicing like she's burning in hell.

Fucking women.

When I look back Salem is in the process of shimmying out of her leather clothes, dropping them onto the floor next to her heels. I thought she was sexy when we first met but now *god, she's sexy and so fucking mine.*

Scars litter her body and I know she gets embarrassed and ashamed of those parts. Especially the one down her inner thigh and the one across her neck.

But I love them.

I love those scars; it proves how strong she is. She survived not only physical abuse from being tortured by the cartel but Luca's men trying to kill her.

Grunting, I strip out of my own clothes tossing them to the side along with hers. Holding out my hand, she follows me into the shower.

Salem sighs when the water hits her skin. "Ahh, this feels great."

"Yeah, like burning in Hell," I mutter, grabbing the sprayer.

"Just means we'll be together." She laughs, closing her eyes as I direct the sprayer over her tits, the water spraying off the blood that somehow got underneath her clothes. Sweeping over her chest, her stomach and down her thighs.

Grabbing a washcloth, I pour body wash and swipe it across her skin, washing her milky scarred skin. By the time I move onto her hair and wash away the blood, I realize Salem hasn't said anything and is being oddly quiet.

"Salem?" Twisting her around, I'm taken back to find tears in her eyes. "Oh, baby, what's wrong?"

"It's done," she mutters, sniffing and shaking her head, as if the emotions are too much for her to feel. She moves back, dropping to her knees before she grabs my cock. I naturally get hard, her small hands wrapping around my base. Before I can protest, she sucks the tip into her mouth, suctioning her cheeks, and takes me into the back of her throat.

"Fuck," I groan, her hands gripping the back of my thighs, nails digging in as she forces me further into her mouth. Gagging, she swallows, her throat muscles convulsing.

"You suck me so well, Kitten." My voice sounds unhuman as I stare down at her on her knees. Her eyes deadlock onto mine, tears forming in her eyes.

These tears are different though. This isn't from sucking my cock, this is something entirely different.

Shit. She's moments from having a full-on breakdown, and she's trying to distract herself or hell even me for that matter.

Pulling her off, I try pulling her to stand up. Only she stops me and falls back onto her butt, her back hitting the shower wall.

"Salem..." Bending down, I reach for her. Shaking her head, a sob breaks from her. Attempting to stop, she bites down on her hand, biting harder than necessary. "Kitten."

Salem shakes her head, tears falling fast then I've seen. And then she screams.

My ears ring.

She screams and screams.

I'm helpless as my arms wrap around her shoulders. I'm completely helpless as the screams for that nine-year-old girl who lost her family to those monsters.

She screams and cries for the parents that never got to watch their little girl grow up.

The siblings she never got to fight and argue with but never protected her from boys like me.

And the little boy she never got to meet but named.

She screams and cries.

3

Salem

I'm losing it.

My mind is a blankness of fog and fuzziness that I can't see straight. My brain hurts, my body aches, and most of all my heart is gone. The biggest part of a human being, the part that makes them whole. Mine is gone. Ripped from my chest and somewhere that I can't find.

I can't cry, the emotions are missing. There's a place deep inside that is gone, unreachable and completely... I'm an empty void.

I'm a black hole that is sucking the life out of myself.

I'm no longer a person. I'm nothing.

I'm no one.

I'm dead.

"Salem!" Zane's voice calls from the stairs.

I open my mouth to say something, but nothing comes out. My throat is raw from screaming. I don't have anything left in me. I'm noth–

"Salem." He's closer now, and then his hand grabs my shoulder. Flinching, my hope that he didn't catch my action isn't possible when he furrows his brows. Confused.

"What happened?" he asks, holding something up. I shrug, not bothering to even look at what he's holding. I don't want to talk. I don't want to feel.

"Don't give me that. What the fuck happened, Salem!" he growls, reaching across the sink and shutting the water off.

When did I turn the water on?

"Shit." He hisses. Why is he hissing at me?

My eyes finally dart down. While one hand is turning red from the water, the other is holding hair.

My hair.

"Answer me, Salem, what did you do?"

I don't know what to say. The words in my head are stuck, and my mouth doesn't work. I'm trapped inside my head, I'm nothing.

"Why did you cut your hair?" he asks. Why is he asking me this?

"Salem, are you getting a haircut like your sister?" Mama asks, fluffing Emmy's hair.

"I like my hair long," I mumble, gripping the end of my waist-length hair. I always had long hair, it's what stood out from Emmy and me. Besides the fact she's a lot older, and taller, and well, beside the fact we're completely different.

I like my hair long.

"That's okay, sweetie, I love your hair long too." Mama kisses the side of my head.

"Emmy, can you braid it?" I nervously ask. It's my favorite thing we do together. She has a way of knowing tons of different braids. French, Dutch, she can even do two.

"Of course!" Emmy smiles, jumping from the stool allowing me to climb up. "What are we going to do this time? Two, maybe I can do two French braids and twist them?"

"Oh, yes! I love that!" I yell with excitement, smiling at my big sister.

"Fucking a girl with short hair is almost like fucking a guy." Giulio laughs, nudging his brother. Emmy screams her voice raw. "At least there's something to grab."

Grunting, skin slapping together, Emmy screaming, and then it is silent.

Everything is silent.

"Blood, pain, screaming, it hurts, everything hurts. Blood, pain, it hurts, their screams, it's loud." I don't even recognize what I'm saying. I can logically think. I'm not completely crazy.

I'm just losing it, losing my mind a bit.

But from the way Zane is staring at me, I've lost it. He's looking at me like I should belong in the hospital. I'm not crazy, I'm just–I'm nothing.

"I'm tired," I mumble, making my way to the stairs. I don't hear Zane. I don't feel. I don't do anything.

I'm supposed to feel better.

Killing him was supposed to heal me, but I'm broken more than I was before.

I'm further broken than I thought possible.

I don't feel the cold that wraps around me; the darkness of my room is my only escape.

My mind is losing itself and all I can do is become the void I'm bound to become.

I was Salem who turned into Ghost and now?

I'm no one. I'm nothing. A void.

4

February

5

March

6

Zion

April

I haven't heard her voice since she told me she was tired and went to our room. I've barely even seen her since then. Besides bringing her three meals that she barely touches, most of the time it's only a bite, maybe half to keep her going, she sleeps and sits in her windowsill.

She's lost.

And I have no idea how to help her.

Salem is no longer there, her eyes are blank, she's not aware of what's happening around her. She's a zombie, a void.

I had to hire help around the farm. Pumpkin has finally gotten used to me riding her around to get in her exercise since Salem hasn't left our room.

Aziza has come over, tried what she thought would work to get her out. But Salem is no longer here. I don't know who's up there lying in her bed, and I have no idea what to do.

I've even gone as far as asking Zion and Izel for help. Izel having a past filled of trauma, and the best advice she has is time. Everyone deals with their issues in their own time. Of course, that's easy for her to fucking say.

Her family was a piece of shit, and she gladly killed her rapist while her brother shot their father.

Salem's family was ripped away from her and the last person that was connected to it is now gone.

She has no idea who she is.

How could she?

The nine-year-old she was, was full of life. She was a farmer with her dad, a baker for her mom, a gamer for her brother, and a hairstylist for her sister.

Then she became Ghost, someone men feared.

Someone I feared.

Then someone I loved.

Until now, now she has no idea who she is, and she's feeling too much too deep and too soon.

She never got to say goodbye.

Aziza told me she never went to their funerals. Hasn't stepped foot in the cemetery.

She's holding on to them coming home.

She's stuck.

She's waiting for you to abandon her too, Zane, Aziza told me. That Salem waits for everyone to leave her, she's waiting for me to give up on her.

Lucky for her, I love the crazy psychopath and I'm a stubborn asshole who has a serious clingy issue to her.

Climbing the stairs, I brace myself for the fight I know she is going to give me. Opening the door, I'm not surprised when I find her sitting in the windowsill looking out into the mountains. Her breakfast is untouched, but her coffee is gone and that gives me hope.

Because I might have drugged it, to try and make moving her a bit easier. Unfortunately for me the closer I look, the coffee is poured on the ground by the bed.

"Let's go for a ride," I attempt and immediately regret it when Salem stands up and narrows her eyes at me.

This is the fight I knew was going to come, but it doesn't prepare me for when she marches up to me, throwing a weak punch. I almost feel bad when I twist her arm and she hisses in pain. Throwing her back to my chest, I miss the connection, and she tries throwing her head back. She's weak from not eating and not working out.

"I'm sorry," I mutter as the needle sticks into her neck. "I love you," I tell her, kissing the back of her head as her body begins to go limp.

"I hate you," she whispers, her eyes rolling to the back of her head, and her body drops. Swiping my arm under her leg, I lift her up. Carrying her downstairs, out to the SUV, I place her in the back seat, before climbing in myself. Hoping I'm not about to make a big mistake and make her worse than she already is.

Fifteen minutes later, I pull into the cemetery. Shutting the car off, I watch Aziza and Killian pull in behind us. My eyes drop down to

Salem, who's currently blinking her eyes open. Her hands rise for what I assume is to rub her head when she realizes they're tied.

I knew she wasn't going to like it, but the death glare I'm receiving has me second guessing my entire life. I almost miss the shadows under her eyes along with her prominent cheekbones.

"Please just remember that I love you," I tell her, shoving myself out the door and opening hers. I nearly miss when she kicks her feet out, and flops onto the cold dirt.

"I hate you," she hisses.

Thank fuck I tied her feet as well. Reaching down, I grab her ankles and begin dragging her towards Aziza and Killian.

"Where's Emilia?" I ask dropping her legs.

"Taylor's watching her. Aziza didn't think it'd be best to bring her." Killian nods towards Salem, who is probably planning all our deaths. I smile at the thought, because at least she'd be doing something. Feeling something besides numb.

"Has Taylor even watched a child before?"

"Not by himself, but we have cameras." Aziza proudly holds up her tablet that displays cameras in literally every room, every corner. And sure enough, Taylor is lying on his chest with Emilia in front of him while he shows her different blocks and toys.

"So, what's the plan?" Killian asks, glancing down at Salem.

"I'm not sure," Aziza says at the same time I say, "She needs to grieve."

"Grieve?" Killian frowns, eyes bouncing between Aziza and I before dropping down to Salem.

"Salem never grieved losing her family, she, well–she, hell– she missed her family's funeral, she never stepped foot in the cemetery," she says, motioning down towards her friend. "She doesn't even know where they're buried."

Killian snaps his head down to her, and Salem tries her best to kick her legs out. All of us take a large step back.

"Where are they..." Killian doesn't have to finish his question, when Aziza points two feet to the left.

Six headstones.

The Gray family, Emily, Andrew, Emmy, Lee, Toby... and Salem.

Salem has her own headstone here.

"Why?" I ask, confused on why she has her own grave here when she didn't die.

Aziza shrugs.

Fuck it, taking out my pocketknife, I make quick work of cutting off the ropes around her feet and hands.

Within seconds, she's twisting my arm so violently I fall, my elbow straining. It's seconds from coming out of its socket. She crawls over me, throwing punches into my stomach. Before I can process what's happening, she's grabbing the back of my head by my hair, smashing my face into her knee.

She's going to kill me.

I'm vaguely aware of Aziza and Killian moving when he yells, "Salem!"

"Don't, he'll stop her if he needs it. But she needs to feel this," Aziza says, reminding me that even if she's seconds away from putting me in the hospital or worse killing me, she's feeling something and I'd rather her beat the shit out of me, then go back to not feeling.

Breathing heavy, she drops my head, and I fall onto my back, trying not to groan and cry in pain. One look at her and I'm shocked to see her chest rising faster and faster, tears streaming down her hollow cheeks.

"You want to know why I have a headstone here, huh?" she yells, her finger slamming into her chest. "Because I died that night too. I died, Zane. I died, okay! They tore me apart; they raped and broke my family apart. They cut and burned me. They KILLED ME THAT NIGHT!" She screams, ripping the neckline of her shirt displaying the gnarly scar across her throat. The one she secretly puts makeup on to try. She doesn't think I notice, but I do.

"Sal–"

"No. I died that night. I don't fucking exist anymore! I don't want to live, I hate myself. I hate that I lived, and that I survived, and they didn't! I should HAVE DIED!"

My heart breaks as she yells, the force of her crying causing her to hiccup. Her ragged breaths come in and she shakes.

"I'm nothing now, I'm a mental case, I'm a fucking void! I'm broken, I'm—there's so much blood, their screams..." Salem sways.

Blood pours from my nose and my head aches but none of that matters. I grab hold of Salem, and just like that night in the shower I hold her in my lap.

"The voices are loud, Zane, make them stop, make them stop," she begs, her eyes red and dark, tears falling down her face onto my shirt. "It hurts, it hurts so much. I hear them screaming. Dada begged them to let us go. Emmy screamed as they tore her apart. I couldn't recognize Lee's face, they destroyed him. Th–they destroyed his face all because he looked like Mama." Salem continues, her voice trembling, hands gripping my shirt so tight like she's afraid if she lets go, I'll disappear. "Mama was the last one," she says, her voice so low I'm sure Aziza and Killian can't hear her. "They made me watch... the blood, the screams... the noises...Zane, the screams, the blood... the blood...You should go, you should leave."

"What?" I'm shocked, confused, and taken aback at her words. She wants me to leave.

Sitting back, she drops my shirt, nodding her head. "Yes, you should leave. I'm no good, I'm nothing. You liked that I was a little crazy, well,

I'm more than a little. My mind is gone, I'm lost and the voices in my head are too loud. So go, leave me." She attempts to remove herself from my lap.

"Don't I get a say in this?" I ask, my eyes snapping to Aziza and Killian who somehow get the word that they should back off. They rush off towards the car. Salem glances back before she once more tries to stand up.

"No, Zane, you don't. You don't get a stupid say. Leave, I don't fucking want you here." Shoving her hands against my chest, I let her up. Shocked that she so easily wants me to leave. *It's the voices in her head.*

Of course, she's trying to make me leave, she doesn't truly want it. But she thinks she's giving me an out, one that I don't want.

Salem backs away, her eyes draining of life again. I won't have it. I'd rather her fight me and hate me than go back to being an emotionless zombie.

I'm on my feet before she realizes what's happening, and I don't give myself time to think before I'm tackling her to the ground. Twisting her around so she's on her back, I grab her hands and force them above her head and straddle her hips. When she was at her strongest, she might have been able to buck me off, but now that she's skin and bone, she has no such luck.

"Get off me," she growls, her eyes warring between the fight and wanting to hide away again.

"You think you're just going to get rid of me?" I ask, unsure of where I'm heading with this.

"I'm trying, yet you're not understanding. Get off me, I don't want you here." As much as she tries, there's no heat in her voice. It's as if she's silently begging me to do anything but that.

"If you run, I'm running with you. Don't you get it, you're not getting rid of me." Before I can think too much into it, I'm grabbing my pocketknife and flicking it open. Salem's eyes widen slightly before they narrow. "You hate that they scared you, you hate that they took your family away from you. You hate everything, including me."

Dragging her shirt up, I try to ignore her ribs that are sticking out. Her stomach is littered in scars, some from when she was nine and others from her revenge path.

She's so fucking beautiful.

"You think you'll escape me." I know I'm sounding like a crazy person. I'm even second guessing my decision when she bucks her hips, eyes flaring the moment the tip of my blade touches her hip. "You're never getting rid of me," I tell her, dragging the blade across her skin. Salem screams, my ears ring, and I just hope no one hears her. I'd probably get arrested, and Dimitri would not like that.

I carve into her skin, blood dripping down her stomach landing in the grass. By the time I'm done, Salem has stopped screaming. I think she passed out. But when I finally look up, not only is she crying, but she's feeling everything.

"You're not getting rid of me Salem, I don't care what you think, what the voices tell you. You're stuck with me, even if that means drugging you and tying you up. Even if that means taking you away, where no one, even your best friend, won't find us. You're not *getting rid of me.*" Licking the carving I inflicted on her hip, the metallic flavor fills my mouth, and groaning, I smile up at her knowing my teeth are stained red.

"If you think you're the only one who's a *little* crazy, I'll gladly meet your crazy with mine. Because it's me and you, Salem, me, and you." Crawling up her body, I grip her chin, bending down until there's only an inch between our faces. "So, if you want to die, if you want to put yourself into the cold fucking ground you better take me with you because I'm not staying in this world where you're not there anymore. Rip that beating organ out of my chest because it belongs to you, it's been yours and it'll stay yours even in death."

Salem cries, twisting her wrist, until I finally give way. I brace myself for her punches, but they don't come. Grabbing the side of my face, she smashes our lips together. Tasting her again is the highlight of my life, loving the taste of her mouth.

It ends too soon. She pushes against my face stopping me from going further.

"Thank you," Salem, my girl, whispers running her fingers through my dirty blond hair.

"You don't need to thank me, Kitten, I'm not going anywhere," I remind her.

"Don't leave me," her voice is rough with emotions. "Please, please just don–"

"I'm not going anywhere." Sitting up, I drag her into my lap. "I'll glue myself to you if I need to." I don't know how I would even do that, but what's that saying, "if there's a will, there's a way."

"I'm sorry," Salem mumbles, pushing her face into my neck. "I'm sorry."

"For what?"

"The way I was treating you, the way I was acting. I just, I wasn't myself."

Rubbing her back, I scoot us back until I'm leaning against one of the gravestones, I'm not sure whose.

"Tell me about it."

"Everything hurts, Zane. I thought I would get better. That I would... I don't know, find myself. I thought I would know what to do, but the more I thought about it, I just, I don't know who I am, Zane." Picking her head up, she looks so sad. So lost.

"Who do you want to be? When you were growing up, what did you want to be?"

Shrugging her shoulders, she barely glances behind me before darting her eyes back to me. I don't know how she has anymore tears left in her, but I guess it's from not grieving.

"How do you have a gravestone here if you didn't know where they were buried?"

Turning her body, she places her head against my chest. "When Uncle Walker had the funeral for them, I was finally out of the hospital. I refused to go, I couldn't face what happened, I didn't want to face the people in this town. But I told him when he was leaving that it felt like I died that night too, that I might as well have. When he came back, he told me I was right, that I did die and if I wanted to be buried with them that he could make it happen. Now I was confused for a nine-year-old, well ten at this point. So, he had them put my stone up there as well, that way if *they* ever did investigate, making sure we were dead, there'd be six headstones. And so, when I do actually *die,* I'll be back with my family."

It all made sense, that's why Luca never figured out who was coming after him. Because if he ever did investigate the Gray family it appeared Salem truly died that night. It was sad, but smart.

"I don't know who I am without my family or without hunting those monsters down," she finally mutters.

"You're young, Salem, you still have time. And just because they're gone doesn't mean you can't still do what you did with them. Who taught you to bake?"

"Mama..."

"And who taught you about the farm?"

"Dada..."

"Do you get what I'm saying?" I ask, kissing the side of her head.

"I do."

"And any time you get that murderous urge, I'm sure Dimitri wouldn't mind you coming with me to hunt them down." That's a lie, there is barely any love between them. It's more of an understanding. Salem will and has done everything for his son Tobias.

"Thank you for not giving up on me."

"Never."

7

Salem

I'm not okay, something inside me is broken, a missing piece inside. My heart hurts, the air I breathe burns my lungs, and the voices in my head refuse to leave. The screams, the begging, the sight of their blood makes my skin crawl.

I can't escape the noise, no matter what I do, it's loud and they won't ever leave me alone. I hear Mama and Dada begging and crying, the *sounds.*

"Let them go!" Mama begs. "Please let them go! They're innocent, just p-please let them go!"

My arms hurt, they're tied so tight. I don't understand. I don't understand what these monsters want. Why are they here? Mama and Dada know them, called him... called him Luca.

"Please, I'm begging you to let the children go," Dada grunts out somewhere behind me, but I can't see him. I try to turn my head, but one of them smacks me and laughs. The pain, everything hurts. The rope is cutting into my wrists, cutting into my legs. Why are they doing this?

They laugh and laugh, and Emmy screams somewhere. My ears ring, I can feel my body shake, and everything burns. I don't understand.

It hurts. My leg hurts, why does my leg burn?

The blood, the screams, everything hurts...

"Salem?" His voice is an angel, bringing me back to the present. His arms wrap around my middle, holding my arms against my chest. I don't know when I started to feel safe in his arms, but it's a feeling I'm just starting to get used to. "Salem?" He repeats my name.

"Hmmm?" Closing my eyes, I lean the back of my head against his chest.

"You were talking and stopped mid-sentence," he says, nudging the side of my neck with his nose.

"I'm so–"

Twisting me around, I'm lifted onto the kitchen counter, spreading my thighs so he can fit between them. "We've talked about this before," he grunts out, no heat in his voice.

"I know," I mumble. Zane and his damn talks. Suddenly I have a mental breakdown and all this man wants to do is talk. Talk about my feelings, talk about the damn sun and fucking moon.

"The voices?"

It's always the voices, and even thinking about how I can hear them makes me feel and sound crazy. But Zane never once makes me feel that way. Instead, he loves me either way. He doesn't make me feel crazy or that I'm a psychopath like the others have called me.

I know I have issues. I know there's something wrong with me. But Zane doesn't treat me as if I am.

"It's just hard." My voice is small. I'm back to being that nine-year-old again.

"I know," he says, giving me a sad smile. My eyes drop, taking in his black dress shirt, black slacks, and dress shoes. It's the first time I've ever seen him dress up, and I hate the reason for it.

"Does it ever get better?" I don't know why I'm asking. Zane didn't have a good relationship with his parents. But he must feel something. I mean, they were his parents after all.

"No." I shouldn't be shocked about his answer, but I am. "But you learn how to deal with the pain, you learn how to deal with the tightness in your chest when you think about them."

"I don't think I'll ever get used to it..."

"We'll figure it out, Salem, no matter what. I'm not leaving, okay?"

All I can do is nod. I don't trust myself to not cry and I know once I start, I'm not going to be able to stop. It's been a month since he drugged me, tied me up, and dragged me to my family's gravesite. To say it was hard to confront those memories and to see where they've been for the past fourteen years is an understatement.

And now I'm going back.

To have a funeral for them and... myself.

"Come on." Grabbing my hips he helps me down from the counter. Taking my hand in his, he leads me out to our car. I try my best to shut the noise off, to think about everything else but them. The whole drive to the cemetery Zane holds my hand.

I can't shake the feeling. I can feel myself losing it again. And now I'm going to lose it in front of everyone. It's not until we've parked that the first sob breaks through.

Zane

Salem sits in the middle of the gravestones, her sobs filling the cold, quiet morning. Killian holds Aziza while she cries silently, her shoulders shaking while she clutches his dress shirt.

My parents' funeral was simple and small. A few other doctors showed up, and most of their pagers went off over a dozen times. I stood there awkwardly while the priest talked on and on about their work, about how wealthy they were. I ended up tuning most of what he was saying out. After that I left and haven't thought about them much since.

So, watching Salem sit in front of her parents' gravesite, crying and begging for them to come back, something unfamiliar awakens inside and I find myself sitting behind her. Dragging Salem against my chest, I circle my arms around her.

"I'm right here," I remind her, my lips pressing against the top of her head.

"It hurts," she sobs.

"I know, baby, I know. I'm right here, I'm right here."

And that's how I spend the day, holding Salem well into the night as she sobs into my chest, until she can't cry anymore. The only time she stopped crying was when she fell asleep.

Picking her up, I get us back to the house and up to bed. Changing out of my dress clothes, I start to remove her funeral clothes when she slowly wakes.

"Shit," she mumbles, realizing we're back home.

"Shhh." Pressing my lips against the scar on her inner thigh, I drag her tights down, leaving her naked.

"Thank you," she whispers.

"You don't need to thank me." Kissing up her scarred leg until I reach her hips when she drags my head, forcing me to look up at her.

"Zane," she says, getting my attention. "I'm not saying thank you because you're helping me heal. I'm, I'm saying thank you for everything. For loving me, for not going back to Russia, for staying on this farm. I just, I love you."

"You're the greatest part of me, Salem, that'll never change. So, break down, fight me, I'm always down for a fight. I told you. You're not getting rid of me no matter what."

"No matter what." Salem smiles, dragging my mouth to hers. Her tongue invades my mouth, giving me everything. Fuck, I've missed her. Fuck, I've missed this.

"Salem…" Pulling away, I try not to push her too much.

"No, don't. I miss you. I need you. I need you too much."

I can't deny her, nor could I resist her. Not when she's giving me those eyes, her bottom lip sticking out, and most of all not when she hooks her legs around my hips pulling me down.

"I love you," I tell her.

And I tell her over and over again, never letting her get inside her head. Only when she's finally asleep, do I drag her body so close there's no space between us. Brushing my finger through her now short hair, Salem sighs in her sleep.

Even if I can't stop the nightmares, I can at least be there for her when they wake her. No matter what she's my little kitten, and no matter what I won't let her fall down that hole again.

She's my reason for being, reason for living, and if she dies, I'm nothing. I might as well die with her.

"I love you, Kitten," I tell her again.

And that's how I spend our nights, keeping her close, reminding her that I love her.

Even if she's psychologically at war with herself, I'll love her through it.

ACKNOWLEDGEMENTS

I need to thank you the **readers,** without you reading Psychological War and giving Salem a voice I wouldn't be here today. I probably never would have published a book if it weren't for you and Salem letting me tell her story.

About the Author

Ryan Mundy is a twenty-five year old, living in South Carolina. But often traveling to Michigan. If she's not busy writing from the voices in her head, she's reading or rewatching shows she's obsessed with.

Keep up to date:

instagram: authorryanmundy

TikTok: @authorryanmundy

Website: https://www.ryanmundywrites.com/

For signed copies check website

Ryan Mundy xoxo